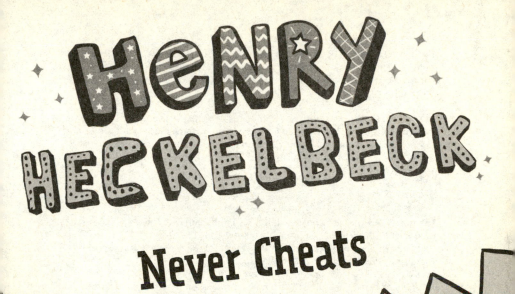

Henry Heckelbeck

Never Cheats

By **Wanda Coven**

Illustrated by **Priscilla Burris**

LITTLE SIMON

New York London Toronto Sydney New Delhi

LITTLE SIMON
An imprint of Simon & Schuster Children's Publishing Division
1230 Avenue of the Americas, New York, New York 10020
First Little Simon paperback edition December 2019
Copyright © 2019 by Simon & Schuster, Inc.
Also available in a Little Simon hardcover edition.
All rights reserved, including the right of reproduction in whole or in part in any form. LITTLE SIMON is a registered trademark of Simon & Schuster, Inc., and associated colophon is a trademark of Simon & Schuster, Inc.
For information about special discounts for bulk purchases, please contact Simon & Schuster Special Sales at 1-866-506-1949 or business@simonandschuster.com. The Simon & Schuster Speakers Bureau can bring authors to your live event. For more information or to book an event contact the Simon & Schuster Speakers Bureau at 1-866-248-3049 or visit our website at www.simonspeakers.com.
Designed by Leslie Mechanic
Manufactured in the United States of America 1119 MTN
10 9 8 7 6 5 4 3 2 1
Library of Congress Cataloging-in-Publication Data
Names: Coven, Wanda, author. | Burris, Priscilla, illustrator.
Title: Henry Heckelbeck never cheats / by Wanda Coven ; illustrated by Priscilla Burris.
Description: First Little Simon paperback edition. | New York : Little Simon, 2019. | Series: [Henry Heckelbeck ; 2] | Summary: When new student Max challenges Henry for the position of goalie on the soccer team, he must decide whether using the *Book of Spells* would make him a cheater.
Identifiers: LCCN 2019017916 | ISBN 9781534461079 (hc) | ISBN 9781534461062 (pbk) | ISBN 9781534461086 (eBook)
Subjects: | CYAC: Magic—Fiction. | Soccer—Fiction. | Schools—Fiction. | Friendship—Fiction. | Brothers and sisters—Fiction.
Classification: LCC PZ7.C83393 Hqn 2019 | DDC [Fic]—dc23
LC record available at https://lccn.loc.gov/2019017916

CONTENTS

Chapter 1

HEY, GOALIE!

Henry Heckelbeck pulled a round sandwich out of his lunch box. Mom had made it with a cookie cutter. Henry showed his best friend, Dudley.

"What does THIS look like?"

Dudley smiled. "It looks like a soccer ball to me!"

"RIGHT!" Henry said. "And today we have the first soccer practice after school!"

Then he held up his free hand, and Dudley smacked it.

Max Maplethorpe heard the boys as she walked by.

"What are you talking about?" she asked.

"Soccer," Dudley said.

Max sat down. "Do you play?" she asked.

Dudley's mouth fell open.

"Well, OF COURSE I play!" he said. "And for your information, I am a center back. My position tries to stop the other team from . . ."

Max held up her hand like a stop sign. "I know. I know," she said.

"You try to stop the other team from scoring a goal."

Dudley was surprised. "Do YOU play soccer?"

Max looked up from under the brim of her baseball cap. "I played goalie at my old school."

Henry smiled. "Hey, goalie!" he exclaimed. "That's what *I* play."

Max didn't say "that's cool" or anything at all. She just stared at Henry.

Henry swallowed hard. "Well, um, soccer sign-ups are at practice after school. Maybe you should join us?"

Max shrugged. "Maybe," she said.

Then she picked up her tray and walked off.

Chapter 2

POP!

The final bell rang. Henry and Dudley grabbed their backpacks and ran to the boys' locker room.

"Do you think Max will try out?" Henry asked.

Dudley slipped a shin guard inside his long sock.

"Who knows?" he said. "But just in case—PLAY YOUR BEST."

A funny feeling swept over Henry. *Dudley's right,* he thought. *What if Max is a really good goalie? What if SHE gets to play goalie and not ME?*

When Henry finished getting dressed, he joined the other kids on the field.

Principal Pennypacker stood on the sidelines in his soccer gear. The principal used to play goalie when he was in school.

Another grown-up was there.
It was Mrs. Noddywonks, the
drama teacher. She
had on a red track
suit and wore
a baseball cap
on top of her
curly orange
hair. A whistle
hung around her
neck.

"Welcome, soccer players!"
Principal Pennypacker said.
"This year, Mrs. Noddywonks
is going to coach our soccer
team. Now you can call her
Coach!"

The kids clapped and whistled because everyone *loved* Mrs. Noddywonks.

Meanwhile, Henry saw that Max wasn't there.

His funny feeling popped like a soap bubble. *Now I'LL get to be goalie for sure!*

Chapter 3

UH-OH!

Coach blew her whistle. "Choose a partner and grab a ball. It's time for warm-ups!"

Henry and Dudley came together like magnets and took a black-and-white ball.

"Start with toe taps," said Coach. She placed a soccer ball in front of her. Then she tapped the  top of the ball with the toes of her cleats. First one foot, and then the other.

Each pair took turns toe-tapping a soccer ball.

"Now let's work on passes,"

Coach directed. "There are four steps to kicking a soccer ball.

"First you must approach the ball. Then you plant your non-kicking foot beside the ball.

Then you strike the ball
with the inside of your other
foot. And finally, you follow
through."

Coach passed the ball to
Principal Pennypacker.

Henry and Dudley passed
the ball back and forth. They
didn't miss once—until Henry
saw Max walk onto the field.

The ball whizzed past Henry. "Dude, wake up!" Dudley cried.

Henry ran after it. That's when he overheard Coach offer to be Max's partner.

Henry turned away and kicked the ball super hard to Dudley. It blew past him.

While Dudley chased after the ball, Henry spied on Max.

She had a very powerful kick. She stopped the ball really well too.

Soon the whistle blew. The players gathered around Coach.

"Okay, team! It's time for a practice game!" she said. "Who wants to play goalie?"

Henry raised his hand as high as it would go. So did Max. Then that funny feeling rushed over Henry again.

Why does Max have to like playing goalie so much? he wondered.

Chapter 4

GOALIE MOLY!

Henry and Max followed Principal Pennypacker to one of the goals for a quick and easy warm-up.

First the principal went over the rules of being a goalie.

"The lines around the goal form the penalty area," he began. "Inside this box, you can use any part of your body to stop the ball. Once you stop the ball, you have six seconds to throw or kick the ball back into play. If the ball goes out of play *behind* the goal, the goalie is awarded a goal kick."

Then Principal Pennypacker stood in goal.

"Always be in the ready position," he went on. "Stay on your toes and watch the ball move across the field. To catch the ball, hold your hands high in a W position.

And always keep your hands
on *top* of the ball."

Principal Pennypacker went
to bounce the ball. He kept his
arms stretched out in front of
him. He caught the ball with
his hands on top of the ball.

Henry watched closely. But Max acted like she knew everything already about goalkeeping. She just twirled her ponytail.

"Henry, you can go first," Principal Pennypacker said. "I'll try to score."

Henry stood in the goal.

Then the principal took a shot,
and Henry blocked it with his
hands.

"Very good," he said. "Now
you try, Max."

Max traded places with
Henry.

The principal dribbled the ball in and kicked. Max slid to one side and saved the ball with her foot.

"Well done!" the principal exclaimed.

Then Henry stepped back in the goal. He wanted to do even better this time.

The principal kicked a bouncy shot. Henry dove for it, but the ball swooshed into the back of the net.

"Nice try!" Max said as she stepped over Henry to take his place.

This time the principal kicked the shot high.

Max tapped the ball away easily with her fingertips.

Henry's jaw dropped. Max was a really good goalie. She might even be better than he was.

Chapter 5

Boo-Boos

Coach divided the players into two teams. Henry went in goal for Team Blue. Max went in for Team Red.

Each team had five players on the field in total.

Team Blue kicked off the game. All the kids chased after the ball. They moved up and down the field like a swarm of bees.

"Spread out! Spread out!"
Coach shouted.

Dudley broke free of the
swarm. He dribbled the ball
and booted it toward the net.
The ball shot by Max.

Score!

Coach blew her whistle. "Nice work!" she said. "Now everybody back in position!"

This time Team Red kicked off. They dribbled the ball into Henry's zone and took a shot.

Henry dove for it and missed.

This time Team Red cheered.

"One to one!" Coach called

out. "Tiebreaker wins!"

Henry wiped the
dirt off his knees
with his gloves.

It was back
to Team Blue, but
Team Red stole the ball.
Then a girl with long braids
kicked it out of bounds behind
the goal line.

Coach blew
her whistle.
"Goal kick!"

Henry tried to kick the ball
to Dudley, but he slipped and
knocked the ball into his own
net. The point counted.

Max yelled, "Team Red
wins!"

Henry lay down on the field.
Dudley ran over and helped
him up.

"It was only a PRACTICE
game!" Dudley said. "So who
cares?"

Henry groaned.

"I bet a joke will help," Dudley said. "What position does a ghost play in soccer?" Henry shrugged.

Dudley smiled. "He plays a really bad GHOUL-ie! Get it? He misses every shot because the ball goes right THROUGH him!"

Henry rolled his eyes and said, "In OUR game, *I* made all the boo-boos. . . . Get it? Ghosts? BOO! BOO!"

Dudley cracked up, and hearing his laugh made Henry feel a little better.

Chapter 6

SISTERLY ADVICE

Back at home Henry knocked on his sister's door. "Will you help me practice my goalie skills?"

"Why would I want to do THAT?" Heidi asked.

Henry bounced his soccer ball on the floor. "Because you can kick soccer balls at me as hard as you want."

Heidi smiled like the Grinch.
"When you put it that way,"
she said, "how can I refuse?"

In the backyard Henry told
Heidi about Max.

"She's new, and she's a really
good soccer goalie," Henry
said. "I'm worried she is better
than me."

Heidi kicked a pine cone for practice. "What's her name?" she asked.

"Her name is Max," he said. "Max Maplethorpe."

Heidi stopped and stared at Henry. "As in MELANIE MAPLETHORPE?"

"They are cousins," said Henry, and Heidi shrieked with laughter.

"If Melanie played goalie, she would need to be the star of the show!" Heidi said.

Henry folded his arms. "Max isn't like that," he said. "She's the OPPOSITE of Melanie. And she's a REALLY good goalie."

Heidi shook her head in disbelief.

"I'm not even kidding," Henry said as he set up the goal.

His sister stood over the soccer ball. "Well, YOU'RE a really good goalie too," she said.

Henry huffed. "But I still need to get better."

Heidi kicked the ball again and again. They practiced until Mom called them in for dinnertime.

As they cleaned up, Heidi
nudged Henry. "Do you want
some big sister advice?"

Henry nodded.

"Don't try to be BETTER than Max," she told him. "Just be the best Henry you can be. And, PS, you're a pretty good Henry Heckelbeck."

Henry bumped his sister back.

"Thanks," he said.

Chapter 7

CHEATER KEEPER

Henry couldn't wait to try his soccer moves at practice. Working with his sister had really helped.

"May I go first today, Coach?" Henry asked.

Coach gave him a double thumbs-up.

Henry jogged to the goal. *Be brave and throw yourself at the ball,* he told himself.

Coach kicked the ball. Henry planted his right foot. He pointed his knee toward the ground. Then he collapsed on the ball and held it tight.

"Well done!" Coach said.

Then she kicked a shot at
Henry's waist. Henry caught
the ball against his chest.

"Wow!" the rest of the team
exclaimed.

Henry made three more solid
saves. Then it was Max's turn.

Max dove for the first ball, but it bounced off her fingertips and into the goal.

"Good try," Coach said.
"Here's another."

Max stood in the ready position with her knees bent and hands up.

The ball came right to her, but she didn't bend over enough. The ball bounced off her chest. She kicked the dirt in anger.

During the practice game, Henry had a shutout for Team Blue, and Max let in three goals for Team Red.

Max was so mad after the game that she yelled, "Henry CHEATS!"

Max's teammates didn't like losing either.

"Yeah!" they shouted.

Coach blew her whistle
sharply.

"Stop that!" she said firmly.

"We are all on the *same* team.

Let's focus on our first real game that is coming up against Frost Elementary."

Max made a sour face at Henry and whispered, "Cheater!"

Henry balled his fists. "AM NOT!" he shot back.

Then Henry and Max stormed off in different directions.

Chapter 8

SOCCER TRICK

Henry ran upstairs to his room, flopped onto his bed, and screamed into his pillow.

There was a knock on his door. It was Dad. "What's wrong?" he asked.

Henry rolled over. "Max called me a CHEATER at soccer today," he said. "And I NEVER cheat!"

Dad sat on the edge of the bed. "Of course you don't," he said. Then he explained that sometimes friends say mean things when they're embarrassed or mad.

Henry thought about it. Max
had been really upset.

Henry sighed. "I guess."

Dad smiled. "So you're
good?"

Henry nodded, and Dad left the room.

But that still doesn't give Max the right to call me a CHEATER, Henry thought.

Then he noticed
something on the
bed beside him. It
was that weird old
book with the letter
M on it.

He popped out the
medallion and set it aside.

 Suddenly the
book jumped into
his hands and
opened all by itself.

The pages fluttered until they came to a stop on a page with a picture of a soccer ball. Underneath it was a spell.

How to Do a Soccer Trick

Have you ever known a poor sport in soccer? Perhaps you've played a really good game and then a member of the opposite team calls you a mean name. If you think you've been treated unfairly, then this is the soccer spell for YOU!

Ingredients:
1 pair of outgrown pants
3 Red Hot candies
1 glass of water
1 toy whistle

Mix the ingredients together in a bucket. Place one hand on your medallion and place your other hand over the mix. Chant the following words.

Liar, liar, pants on fire!
Time to make another call!
From now on [person's name]
will FEAR the ball!

Note: Payback spells rarely work out the way one thinks. Kindness breaks the spell.

A smile spread across Henry's face. Maybe it was time for a little magic.

Henry gathered the ingredients and chanted the spell.

Sparkles swirled from the bucket.

Suddenly Henry couldn't wait till tomorrow's game.

Chapter 9

BREWSTER VERSUS FROST

The Frost Elementary team arrived right after school. Everyone warmed up on the field.

"Max, you'll start in goal," Coach said.

Henry folded his arms. *Why does MAX get to start?* he wondered.

Then Henry remembered the spell. If it worked, then he would be goalie in no time.

Brewster had the ball first. They kept it in the offensive zone far away from Max. Dudley cross-kicked the ball in front of the net.

With a slide, the Frost goalie saved the shot! Then she kicked the ball. It whizzed by all the players and headed right to Max.

Max waited eagerly, but then the spell kicked in. *Zing!* When the ball reached her, Max squealed and jumped away. The ball slowly rolled into the goal. Frost had scored.

Henry covered his mouth to hide a laugh. The game restarted, and Frost stole the ball. A boy with spiky hair kicked it toward the goal.

Max didn't try to catch the ball. She *dodged* it! The ball smacked into the back of the net. Frost scored again!

The Brewster players were upset. Everyone except Henry.

Finally the whistle blew for halftime. Poor Max ran off the field and hid.

Ha! Now it's my turn! Henry thought. *Time to save the day!*

Chapter 10

A BAD SPELL

"Your turn in goal, Henry,"
Coach said. Henry hopped up
from the bench. Then he saw
Max. She was sitting all by
herself. Tears streamed down
her cheeks.

Wow, she's REALLY sad, Henry realized. *And it's all MY fault.*

Then he remembered his sister's advice: *Just be the BEST Henry you can be.*

Henry hung his head. He had not been a very good Henry at all.

He walked over to Max. She rubbed her eyes and looked up at Henry.

"What are you going to do?"
she asked. "Make fun of me?"
Henry shook his head.

"Actually, I just want you to know that you're an awesome goalie," he said. "Everybody has a BAD SPELL once in a while."

Then Henry called the team over. "Everyone, I have something to say. Max is a really good goalie who had

some bad luck. But we NEED her right now. Max is the one who should be in goal."

Coach smiled and asked if Max still wanted to play.

"You can do it," Henry told her. "I KNOW you can."

"I'll do it," said Max.

The Brewster players all clapped for their goalie.

Henry sat back down on the bench. Principal Pennypacker slid beside him.

"Seems you have a *magical* gift for coaching," he said.

Before Henry could answer, a Frost player kicked the ball on goal. Max dove for it and grabbed the ball out of the air. It was a spectacular save! The spell had been broken!

The crowd cheered, but Henry cheered the loudest. It felt good to be the best Henry he could be.

Check out the next book starring

HENRY HECKELBECK

HENRY HECKELBECK
and the Haunted Hideout

"I spy an anthill," said Dudley Day. He was Henry Heckelbeck's best friend. Dudley watched the ants scurry in and out of the hole. He wondered about the secret tunnels inside.

An excerpt from *Henry Heckelbeck and the Haunted Hideout*

"I spy a bird's nest!" cried Henry, pointing his binoculars at the treetops.

"Wouldn't a nest make a cool hangout?"

Dudley stood up and said, "Yeah. So would an anthill."

Then Henry spotted a red-orange cat in the garden.

"I spy something FURRY," he whispered. The cat belonged to the next-door neighbors.

An excerpt from *Henry Heckelbeck and the Haunted Hideout*

Henry had nicknamed him Kevin.

Dudley tiptoed to Henry's side. "Let's follow it!" he said.

The boys tracked Kevin along the stone wall and down into Henry's dad's vegetable patch. Kevin stopped and chewed on some spinach.

"Ew!" the boys cried.